LBP

This book belongs to

_____

™

Bully Bean

STORY BY

Thomas Weck *and* Peter Weck

ILLUSTRATIONS BY

Len DiSalvo

LIMA BEAR PRESS, LLC
Wilmington, Delaware

Published by Lima Bear Press, LLC

Lima Bear Press, LLC
2305 MacDonough Rd., Suite 201
Wilmington, DE 19805-2620

Visit us on the web at
www.limabearpress.com

Book & Cover design by: rosa+wesley, inc.

Printed in the USA.

FIRST EDITION
ISBN: 978-1-933872-05-6

Weck, Thomas L., 1942–
    Bully Bean / story by Thomas Weck and Peter Weck ; illustrations by Len DiSalvo. — 1st ed.

    p. : col. ill. ; cm. — (The Lima Bear stories ; [#5])

    Summary: In the kingdom of Beandom, Bully Bean is feared. He makes fun of other beans,
plays mean tricks, and puts others in danger. Lima Bear seems to be Bully Bean's favorite bean
to pick on, perhaps because Lima Bear is the only bean with green fur and is always helping others.
But what will Lima Bear and his friends do when Bully Bean is in danger?
    Interest age level: 003-008.
    ISBN: 978-1-933872-05-6

    1. Bears—Juvenile fiction. 2. Bullying—Juvenile fiction. 3. Helpfulness—Juvenile fiction.
4. Bears—Fiction. 5. Bullying—Fiction. 6. Helpfulness—Fiction. I. Weck, Peter (Peter M.)
II. DiSalvo, Len. III. Title.

PZ7.W432 Bul 2013
[Fic]

Bully **Bean** was the tallest and **strongest** bean in all of Beandom. He liked to tease and torment the other beans. When they saw him, the other beans would chant:

Oh, bad Bully Bean,
   What makes you so **mean**?
Whenever you're near,
   We all **run** in fear.

Bully Bean especially liked to torment Lima Bear because Lima Bear was always kind and good-natured. He was the only bean with green fur, so he was easy to spot.

One time, **Bully Bean** picked up Lima Bear by his fur
and dropped him into a mud puddle. Lima Bear came up all
brown and **wet**. As the other beans cleaned him up and dried
him off, they chanted:

Oh, bad **Bully Bean**,
    What makes you so **mean**?
Whenever you're near,
    We all *run* in fear.

Another time, **Bully Bean** dug a deep hole in the ground and put Lima Bear in it. The hole was so deep that no matter how hard he tried, Lima Bear could not climb out. When **Bully Bean** walked away, the other beans heard Lima Bear crying. They lowered a ladder into the hole so Lima Bear could escape. As he climbed up the ladder, the other beans chanted:

Oh, bad **Bully Bean**,
　　What makes you so **mean**?
Whenever you're near,
　　We all **run** in fear.

Not far from Beandom, there was a hidden cave. It had a small opening that only Lima Bear and the other beans could squeeze through.

Lima Bear liked to explore this underground fantasyland.

He liked to look above his head to find holes in the ceiling of the cave. Light would stream down through these holes. The rays of light made the stalactites that hung from above glisten like icicles. They made the stalagmites that grew on the floor of the cave glow. It was a magical sight to see.

One day, when Lima Bear was alone in the cave, he saw something move near a tall pink-colored stalagmite. It was **Bully Bean**! He had found a secret entrance to the cave. As soon as Lima Bear saw **Bully Bean**, he ran for his life.

Oh, bad **Bully Bean**,
What makes you so mean?
Whenever you're near,
We all *run* in fear.

Lima Bear quickly climbed a rock wall to escape. **Bully Bean** was close behind him. There were lots of loose rocks on the way up, but Lima Bear was so light that they stayed in place.

Bully Bean was not so lucky. One of the rocks he grabbed to climb up the wall came loose. It rolled against his body and trapped him. Try as he might, Bully Bean could not free himself.

"Help me!" Bully Bean called out to Lima Bear. "I'm trapped."

Lima Bear didn't look back. He quickly found the small bean-sized opening and squeezed out of the cave.

Too bad Bully Bean
        You are trapped it would seem.
And who will come here
        To save whom they fear?

It wasn't long before Lima Bear and a team of beans returned to the cave. They worked as fast as they could to free **Bully Bean.** A group of beans fastened a pulley to the ceiling of the cave. Lima Bear and another group of beans tied one end of the rope around the rock. They slowly fed the other end of the rope through the pulley and began to pull. SNAP! The rope broke. It was not strong enough to lift up the rock.

Just then another group of beans entered the cave with three more ropes. Lima Bear braided the ropes together to make a rope cable. It was much stronger and did not break.

Will the beans now be able
    To pull on the cable,
So he can be freed
    By their kindhearted deed?

Alas, the rock was too heavy. The beans were not strong enough to move it.

At Lima Bear's command, the **strongest** beans shinnied up the rope cable and held onto it tight. One by one, the beans grabbed a piece of the rope and shinnied up. Soon the rope looked like a long string of beads.

Finally, as the last bean shinnied up the rope, the rock
moved. The total weight of all the beans was just enough to
loosen the rock so **Bully Bean** could free himself.

Later, when they were safely on the ground, Lima Bear and the other beans looked up at **Bully Bean**. They saw the strangest sight: there were tears in his eyes.

"Why did you come back to save me, Lima Bear?" he asked. "I have been so mean to you."

"Because you're a bean," Lima Bear said. "I had to rescue you."

At first, **Bully Bean** seemed to have nothing to do in Beandom. He no longer bullied anyone. But as he saw how hard the other beans worked to grow food, make new paths and build new homes, **Bully Bean** realized how much he could be of help because of his great size and strength.

Soon, **Bully Bean** was working as hard as all the other beans in Beandom. **Bully Bean** would proudly give Lima Bear a free ride wherever he wanted to go.

The other beans changed **Bully Bean**'s name to **Biggest Bean**. And whenever they saw Lima Bear riding on **Biggest Bean**'s shoulder, they would chant:

Biggest Bean he is so kind.
Upon his shoulder you will find
That Lima Bear is sitting high.
So high that he can touch the sky.

THE END

EXTEND THE LEARNING

Read *Bully Bean*

Before reading, you might:

- Let children know this story is about a bully. Encourage them to share personal experiences they have had with a person who deliberately tries to hurt others. Have children talk about specific things the person did or said and how it made them feel. If appropriate, make a word web. Write the word *bully* in the center circle. Then list related words around the center circle that help to define the word.
- Read the title and briefly discuss details in the cover illustration. Browse through the first few pages. Help children set a purpose for reading, such as *I want to find out how Lima Bear might handle a situation with a bully.*
- *Let's read* Bully Bean *to find out what happens between Lima Bear and Bully Bean.*

During reading, stop and ask children questions to make sure they are following along. Take time to talk about details in the illustrations to help children understand story concepts and unfamiliar vocabulary. Ask questions such as:

- (page 1) *Bully Bean likes to tease and torment the other beans. What do you think* torment *means? Tell me about a time when someone tormented you. How did it make you feel? What did you do?*
- (page 4) *How does the illustration help you understand that Bully Bean is mean?*
- (page 6) *Can you recall how Lima Bear and the other beans get into the cave? Who can find the cave opening in this illustration? What words would you use to describe the cave opening?*
- (pages 12-13) *What happens after the rock traps Bully Bean? How does this affect the story's plot? What do you think Lima Bear will do next?*
- (page 13) *Can you fill in the missing word? Lima Bear quickly found the small bean-sized opening and _____ out of the cave.*

- (page 15) *Why do you think Lima Bear returns with the other beans to save Bully Bean? Would you help Bully Bean? Why or why not?*
- (page 16) *The strongest beans shinnied up the rope. What do you think shinnied means? Can you think of another word that means almost the same thing?*

After reading, take time to talk about the book. You might ask:

- *Tell me what this story is mostly about.*
- *What did you like most about this story?*
- *What words would you use to describe Bully Bean? What would you do if you saw someone being bullied by Bully Bean? Explain your thinking.*
- Write the following words on the board: tease, torment, bully, mean. *Say: Tell me the meanings of each of these words. How do you think these words go together?* Then have children select a word to use orally in a sentence.
- Let's look for details in the story that help you visualize Bully Bean.
- Locate parts of the story that describe how the other beans save Lima Bear from Bully Bean. Ask: *What are some other ways the beans could have helped Lima Bear here?*
- *Lima Bear liked to explore the cave. It was an underground fantasyland. Can you recall specific details that helped you visualize what the cave looked like?*
- Reread the story aloud as a reader's theatre presentation. Take turns reading the narrative text and the rhyming refrains. Talk about ways to change the tone or speed of your voice to make the reading more dramatic. For example, direct children to read lines in the rhyming refrain fast and slow or loud and soft. Have them look for places to pause or to put more emphasis on a particular word (*All the beans ran <pause> in **fear**.*).

ACTIVITIES!

- **Invent a Machine**   Explain how a pulley works and why it's a helpful tool. If possible, bring in a pulley to demonstrate how it works. Make a list of pulley systems found in a home (many blinds use pulleys) or school (flagpoles). Ask children to invent a simple machine that will help people lift things up. Have them draw a picture of their machine and think of a name for it. Then have them explain how their machine works.

- **Learn about Homophones**
Explain that some words sound the same but are spelled differently and have different meanings. These words are called homophones. Locate and list the following words: *would* (page 1), *hole* (page 5), *sight* (page 8), *break* (page 15), and *high* (page 20). Revisit your word list to write a word that sounds the same but has a different meaning.

would   wood

hole   whole

sight   site

break   brake

high   hi

Then ask questions about these words to reinforce word meanings, such as
Which word is a car part?
Which word describes something that might happen to a dish?
Which word is something you would say to a friend?
Which word describes a material used to build a house?
Which word is the opposite of low?

- **Learn about Caves**   Use the internet and other resources to find out how caves are formed over time. List interesting facts about caves, such as different kinds of rock formations (stalagmites, stalactites), animals (bats, cave crickets, eyeless fish), and underground rivers. Work together to define content vocabulary, such as stalagmites and stalactites. Then use the facts and definitions to talk about caves.

- **Make Comparisons**   Use index cards to illustrate sets of words that compare. Begin with the word *strong* to make the first set of cards. Write the word *strong* on one index card. On another card, add –*er* to *strong* to write the word *stronger*. On another card, add –*est* to *strong* to write the word *strongest*. Discuss ideas on how to illustrate the meaning of each word. For example, a strong man, a stronger man, the strongest man. Repeat with *tall* (*taller, tallest*), *small* (*smaller, smallest*), and *big* (*bigger, biggest*). Guide children to notice how adding –*er* means "more" and adding -*est* means "most."

- **Learn about mnemonics**   Explain how mnemonics are memory strategies people use to remember information. Share the following mnemonic to help children remember the difference between stalactites and stalagmites:

    Stalactites hold *tight* to the ceiling.
    Stalagmites *might* grow and touch the ceiling some day.

Encourage children to find or create their own mnemonics to help them remember important information.

This letter from Thomas Weck to his now adult son Peter gives readers a peek into the origination of The Lima Bear Stories that have won national awards including the Peace Corps Book of the Year Award.

Dear Peter,

This is a long overdue letter to thank you for pushing me to share with others the Lima Bear Stories that I made up and told to you and your brother David and sister Kathryn (and, of course, to Andrew, too, later on) when you were all somewhere between three and eight years old.

I can still picture the four of us in the double bed with my arms cuddling the three of you as you all eagerly awaited the story. You all loved the bean-sized characters because, as small children, you could relate your own challenges in coping with an "oversized" world designed for adults to the challenges faced by these tiny beans.

Some of the Lima Bear stories I must have told to you kids at least 10 times. You can imagine my delight when I discovered that all of you seemed just as happy hearing an already-told story over again. You and your siblings would, on occasion, tell some of the stories to each other—a delightful experience for me whenever I witnessed this.

You were always my biggest fan. You would laugh the most, even at a story you had heard many times before. Your laughter was a great tonic to me.

But all this storytelling introduced an unexpected challenge. When I retold a story, sometimes I was unable to recall all of the original details. But you could, and whenever I made a "mistake"—for example, calling King Limalot's robe red when I had originally called it purple—invariably you would correct me. Sometimes, particularly when I was really tired from a hard day at the office, it seemed I made a lot of mistakes. Your corrections became so numerous as to interrupt the flow of the story.

Finally, your exasperated brother, David, would say: "Peter, just let Daddy tell the story. What difference does it make if he called the robe red?"

Kathryn, the born mediator of the family, would then chime in: "But David, it was purple."

I needed a solution, and I needed it pronto. At first, trying to remember every detail of a retold story proved inadequate. Then I latched onto a different strategy. A case in point: as a story came to, say, the color of a robe, I would say: "And the king's robe colored a beautiful...Peter, I bet you remember the color of the robe."

Without a pause, you would advise us all that it was purple.

And I would say: "That's right, purple," and go on with the story. This approach seemed to satisfy all parties.

Luckily, in 2000, you approached me at the age of 29 to volunteer to join forces with me to create a children's book publishing company. You were concerned that the Lima Bear Stories, now fallow, would vanish unless put into print. You began a campaign to prevent this from happening. The idea was that we would each contribute our memories, still vivid, to bring these stories back to life.

It was your persistence that led us into this venture. As I once told you, if you were ever reincarnated as an inanimate object, you would come back as the tide. And we've collaborated ever since. And what a joy it is for me to have this unique relationship with you as we reconstruct the stories. I think both of us are still young at heart, with all the wonderment, curiosity and innocence of children.

Our partnership has warmed me in ways hard to express in words. And as we reconstruct the stories, hearing you laugh all over again with that same infectious laugh as when you first heard these stories motivated me even more and made me glow inside. It has lent to our togetherness as father and son a new, wonderful dimension.

Your memory has surely proved useful as we reconstructed the stories for ultimate publication through our company, Lima Bear Press, LLC. Thanks to you, and to our combined efforts, and also to our team of six professionals, eleven stories are now written, with five published and more to come next year.

Love,

Dad

Go to www.limabearpress.com
for books, activities and more stories about this series.

25

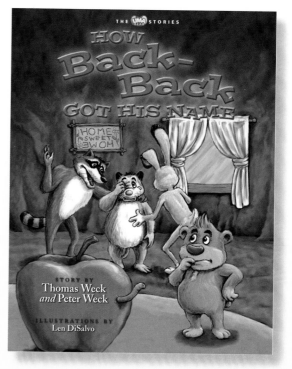

What's the King of Beandom to do? The tiny, multi-colored beans of Beandom are under attack by a monster. Even the King's wisest advisors seem unable to find a solution. Who will save Beandom? Can an ordinary tiny bean step forward with a plan that works?

Welcome to Beandom! It's a great place to visit. Or, it will be—just as soon as we get rid of that pesky monster!

$15.95

Can you imagine what it would be like to lose your back!!? Well, that is exactly what happens to Plumpton, the Opossum. Lima Bear and his clever friends become detectives searching for his missing back. Follow them as they try new and different ways of thinking to solve the mystery. See how they band together to protect each other in times of danger! Will they ever find Plumpton's back?

$15.95

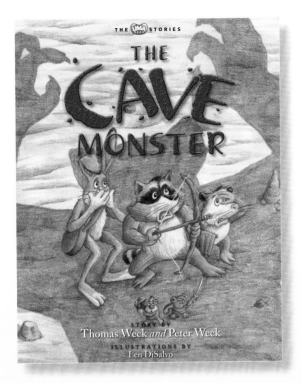

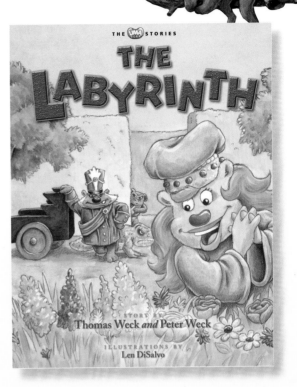

Oh, no!!! L. Joe Bean, Lima Bear's cousin, has been captured by the Cave Monster. The Cave Monster is going to cook L. Joe Bean and eat him. Lima Bear and his friends enter the dangerous Black Cave to save L. Joe Bean. The Cave Monster attacks. Will they save L. Joe Bean in time? And will they save themselves? Read on to see how bravely they fight the Cave Monster.

$15.95

Princess Belinda Bean has just been given the throne by her elderly father. She is now the Queen and the Ruler of Beandom. Everyone is happy about this except the jealous Mean ol' Bean who wants to be the King and Ruler. Mean ol' Bean lures Belinda into a magic labyrinth from which he believes there is no escape. However, L. Joe Bean, the Wiseman of Beandom, discovers the plot. Will he be able to save his Queen? What will happen to Mean ol' Bean?

$15.95

"Authors Tom Weck and Peter Weck, a father-son team, have worked together to fashion entertaining tales drawn from the stories father used to tell his son. The result—clever, engaging, feel-good books with a solid, practical message that will resonate in childhood and beyond."
FAMILYFOCUSBLOG.COM

"...the books are handsome and beautifully illustrated... the Lima Bear stories are winning books, as engaging for children as they are for the parent. It's a different and interesting world that the Wecks create, along the lines of the Smurfs, Care Bears, or Disney's Tinkerbell fairies. The children's attention span at these ages is not great, and it takes a truly engaging story to keep them as riveted as the Wecks' tales do."
TONY D'SOUZA, AUTHOR AND COLUMNIST,
PEACECORPSWORLDWIDE.ORG

"...fascinating stories with messages and morals...This is also a great story from a family and business point of view. I'm glad these stories are being shared."
STEVE ADUBATO, DURING AN INTERVIEW WITH
THOMAS WECK ON "ONE-ON-ONE WITH
STEVE ADUBATO" WHICH AIRED
ON SIX PBS-TV STATIONS

"...engaging and satisfying....Told in a friendly, energetic but thoughtful style... a smart read. DiSalvo's zesty artwork brings to mind a classic, vintage look as in 'Peter Rabbit' and 'The Briar Rabbit.' As a bonus, extra activity and learning ideas bring up the rear of this fun tale."
LEE LITTLEWOOD, KIDS' HOME LIBRARY COLUMN,
CREATORS SYNDICATE

"An adorable children's book that takes kids of all ages on an amazing adventure. It encourages early reading skills with the use of rhymes and gives kids the opportunity to problem solve! LOVE the 'extended learning and activities.'"
JENNIE AND KIM, SURVIVING MOTHERHOOD,
WWW.MOTHERHOODSUPPORT.COM

"Thomas Weck and Peter Weck know what children like. They also have a way of portraying important life lessons through child-friendly characters. *The Cave Monster* is a new favorite. The Lima Bear Stories Series as a whole is one I highly recommend. We are already anxiously awaiting book number four!"
KRISTIN, REVIEWED BY MOM BLOGGER

66...one of the best books you can invest in for your child. It will last, and it teaches many lessons, some might be for when your child is older, so keep it around, and read with them often. After all is said and done, that is the best gift for you and your children—spending quality time with them.99

DAVID BROUGHTON, STORIES FOR CHILDREN MAGAZINE

66There are wonderful messages underlying the fast-paced story. Children will love the example of friends working together and facing challenges even when scared.99

LYDA WHITING, AWARENESS MAGAZINE

66The basic goal for this and the other Lima Bear books is to help children who listen to and/or read them become eager readers throughout their lives.99

WAYNE S. WALKER, BOOK REVIEWER, HOMESCHOOLBLOGGER.COM/ HOMESCHOOLBOOKREVIEW.COM

66Characters are developed nicely...Children will be challenged... Message about forgiveness that provides an additional dimension... All this, combined with bright and engaging illustrations, make it a winner.99

FEATHERED QUILL BOOK REVIEWS

66Additional learning activities and thinking questions help complete the messages and ideas explored... a great book for children ages 4-8. These books should be found in the children's book section of every library in the country.99

JAMES A. COX, MIDWEST BOOK REVIEW, CHILDREN'S BOOKWATCH

66Teaching us messages like tolerance, diversity and courage, the Lima Bear stories are big, colorful, and we love the way they changed the text to reflect the meaning of the word—Megasaurus is printed in big, red, prehistoric-looking type.99

AMY MCCARTHY, PARENTHOOD.COM

To read more reviews, go to
www.limabearpress.com